Lost in Time, A Medieval Adventure

Adapted by Steven Banks
Illustrated by The Artifact Group

SpongeBob and Patrick hurried through Bikini Bottom to get to Medieval Moments restaurant.

"C'mon, Patrick, it's almost time for the joust!" said SpongeBob. The two friends stood before the entrance.

A booming voice played over the castle's speakers. "You're just twenty wizard's paces away from swords, sorcery, and bad hygiene!"

The restaurant's stadium was packed with a cheering audience. The medieval king cleared his throat and spoke into a microphone. "By royal decree, I ask that two people come forth for the royal joust!"

SpongeBob and Patrick waved their hands wildly. "Over here! Pick us!" they cried. The king called them into the arena.

"I can't believe we'll be watching the royal joust from so close up!" SpongeBob said.

"You are not watching the joust," an attendant remarked. "You are *in* the joust!"

SpongeBob and Patrick nervously climbed on to their seahorses. "Mr. Seahorse, sir . . . , you're gentle on beginners, aren't you?" SpongeBob whispered. Suddenly, both seahorses bucked up into the air.

"SpongeBob, HELP!" yelled Patrick. The boys flew off the seahorses and crashed through the wall!

PLOP! SpongeBob and Patrick hit the ground.

"Look, Patrick!" said SpongeBob. An army of knights was charging toward them. "Some employees from the restaurant are coming to help us!"

"Arrest them for committing the act of witchcraft by falling from the sky!" ordered one of the knights. "Taketh them to jail!"

"Wow, they really go the extra mile here!" SpongeBob said.

In the royal dungeon, SpongeBob and Patrick heard a familiar sound . . . it was bad clarinet playing!

"Squidward? What are you doing here?" asked SpongeBob.

"My name is Squidly!" said the prisoner. "I was the royal fool until I told a bad joke and the king locked me up!"

"We really *are* in medieval times!" said SpongeBob. "We must have gone back to the past!"

Suddenly, they felt a rumble in the dungeon. "That is the evil wizard's dragon sent to destroy the king's village," explained Squidly.

Then a guard came and took them all to King Krabs.

"Mr. Krabs?" asked SpongeBob.

"I am the feared ruler of this kingdom!" said the king. "I know you have been sent by Planktonamor to destroy me! It is time for your punishment. Off with their heads!"

"Aaah!" cried SpongeBob and Patrick.

"Wait, Father! Spare them!" the king's daughter, Princess Pearl, begged. "Hast thou forgotten the famous prophecy?"

"What prophecy?" asked King Krabs.

Pearl told the story about how two brave knights were supposed to fall from the sky and slay the dragon of Planktonamor, the evil one-eyed wizard!

"Don't you see? These strangers have been sent to rescue us!" Pearl cried.

Suddenly, a huge jellyfish dragon crashed through the castle and grabbed
Princess Pearl!

"Help me, Father!" screamed Princess Pearl.

"Let go of her, you overgrown amoeba!" shouted King Krabs.

"The evil Planktonamor's dragon has taken Pearl!" cried King Krabs. "And he won't return her until I give him my kingdom!"

"Bummer," said Patrick.

"You two brave knights have been chosen to rescue Princess Pearl!" ordered King Krabs.

"We're ready, Your Majesty!" said SpongeBob.

"And take my fool, Squidly, with you!" added the king.

The trio first stopped at the local blacksmith to get proper armor for the trip. "We have a long journey ahead of us," said Squidly.

SpongeBob reached inside his pocket and pulled out a brown bag. "I always carry some delicious Krabby Patties with me," said SpongeBob. "After we rescue the princess we'll have a snack."

"Ooooh!" said Patrick.

Soon SpongeBob, Patrick, and Squidly came face to face with the fearsome dark knight who guarded the bridge to Planktonamor's castle.

"None shall pass!" the dark knight boomed.

"But, we have to pass, oh scary knight who looks a lot like my friend Sandy," said SpongeBob. "The king has sent us to rescue the fair Princess Pearl from the evil Planktonamor!"

"Thou will haveth to get past me, first!" said the dark knight.

"Hi-yah!" shouted SpongeBob as he karate-chopped her weapon in half.

"What is this strange new fighting technique?" asked the dark knight.

"It is called 'karate,'" said SpongeBob.

"It pleases me!" said the dark knight. The two fought in a series of karate battles and SpongeBob won.

"Since you have bested me in battle and spared my life, I shall let you all cross, and I shall accompany you on your quest!" said the dark knight.

Meanwhile, in the castle of Planktonamor, the evil wizard was celebrating his upcoming victory. "Ha! Ha! Ha! Soon the king's village will be mine! Mine! Mine!"

"That's what you think!" said Princess Pearl. "The prophecy will come true! My rescuers will save me!"

The dark knight helped SpongeBob, Patrick, and Squidly get past the evil wizard's guards. They climbed up the tower stairs to rescue Princess Pearl. "Hang on, Princess Pearl! We're coming to help you!" yelled SpongeBob. "And then we'll eat!" added Patrick.

SpongeBob was determined to stop Planktonamor. "Unhand her, you fiend!" he yelled.

Planktonamor laughed. "Why don't you maketh me?"

"I shalleth!" replied SpongeBob.

"Destroy-eth them, dragon!" ordered Planktonamor.

The giant jellyfish dragon swooped around the castle zapping the intruders.

"I'm afraid this is the end, Patrick!" SpongeBob said, sobbing.

"But I want my Krabby Patty!" cried Patrick.

"Good idea!" said SpongeBob, pulling them out.

Just as Patrick was about to take a bite, the dragon took the food with its tentacle!

"Look! The dragon's eating the Krabby Patty!" exclaimed SpongeBob.

"Hey, dragon!" yelled Planktonamor. "What part of destroyeth dost thou not understand?"

The giant dragon ignored its master and happily kept munching away.

"We defeated the dragon!" shouted SpongeBob.

"Curses!" said Planktonamor. "Foiled by a Krabby Patty!"

King Krabs threw a royal parade for the new heroes. "For your reward, brave knights, I shall give you my two prize seahorses!" said King Krabs.

SpongeBob and Patrick got on the seahorses and began to ride. Suddenly, the horses lost control, and SpongeBob and Patrick were bucked up into the sky!

"Hey! Wake up you guys!" said the Medieval Moments waiter. "You fell on your heads and got knocked out!"

"Wow, Pat!" said SpongeBob. "That was some dream!"

"So, can we eat now?" asked Patrick.